The Adventures of Fudgie the Chocolate Labrador

Written and Illustrated
By Roseanne Fleischman

ISBN 1-4196-4462-9

To order additional copies, please contact us.
BookSurge, LLC
www.booksurge.com
1-866-308-6235
orders@booksurge.com

To my wonderful parents, my loving husband and child and my entire family. Thank you for all of your support and encouragement -R.F.

My name is Craig Scott and I live
in the beautiful Pocono Mountains
of Pennsylvania in the good old U.S.A.
This is my wonderful dog named
Fudgie, Fudgie the Chocolate Labrador.

You are probably wondering if Fudgie is really made of chocolate. Unfortunately he is not. Sorry to disappoint you. But if you use your imagination he sometimes looks like a tasty chocolate layered cake or even a yummy chocolate Easter Bunny or a giant Hershey's Kiss or...well you get the picture.

CHOCOLATE
EASTER
BUNNY

There are many wonderful qualities that make Fudgie
so special. Let me begin by saying that he is very
loyal and always friendly.

Secondly, unlike me Fudgie never complains about doing chores around the house. For example, he loves to help Dad collect wood for the fire.

Fudgie even enjoys helping Mom carry in the
groceries from the truck. He is such a nice dog.

Fudgie also has a fun side. For example, in the summertime Fudgie loves to go swimming in the lake. He is a very good swimmer.

Sometimes Fudgie just likes to lie in the grass and smell the flowers. He is such a sweet dog.

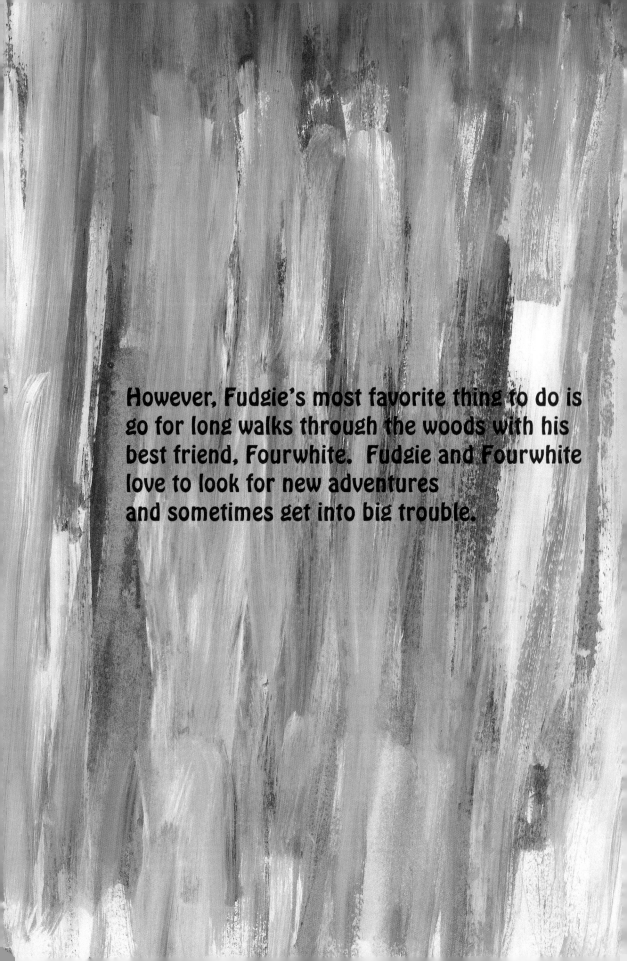

However, Fudgie's most favorite thing to do is go for long walks through the woods with his best friend, Fourwhite. Fudgie and Fourwhite love to look for new adventures and sometimes get into big trouble.

One bright and sunny day Fudgie and Fourwhite decided to go for a long walk through the woods. As they were strolling along they heard a strange noise. It sounded like a cry coming from the bushes. When they got closer they realized it was a little bunny rabbit stuck in a hunter's trap.

Fudgie and Fourwhite got right to work. First Fudgie began to gnaw at the rope with his sharp teeth then Fourwhite used his powerful hind legs to kick the trap open. In a few minutes the sweet little bunny was set free and hopped away with a smile.

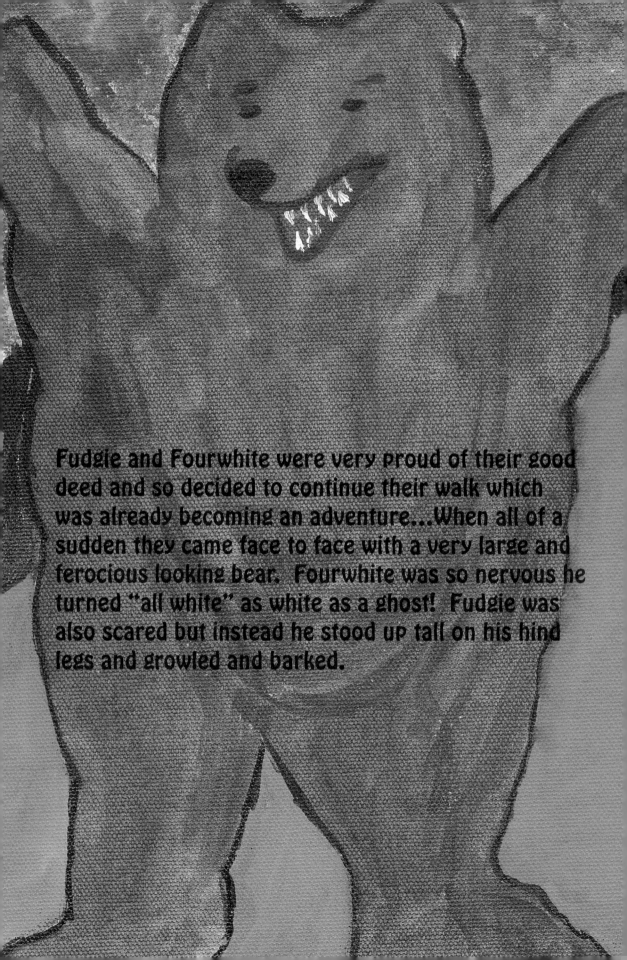

Fudgie and Fourwhite were very proud of their good deed and so decided to continue their walk which was already becoming an adventure...When all of a sudden they came face to face with a very large and ferocious looking bear. Fourwhite was so nervous he turned "all white" as white as a ghost! Fudgie was also scared but instead he stood up tall on his hind legs and growled and barked.

The bear was startled and ran away. Hooray for Fudgie! He is such a brave dog.

Meanwhile, Fudgie was so excited to have scared the bear away he didn't notice that Fourwhite had disappeared. Fudgie called out to his best friend but Fourwhite was nowhere to be found. So Fudgie began to cry. He was worried he would have to walk home all alone.

All of a sudden...Fourwhite came running out of the
bushes. Apparently, while hiding from the bear he
had fallen asleep. Boy was Fudgie glad to see his
friend. They both decided it was getting late and
time to go home. What an adventurous day!

I hope you have enjoyed the story of my wonderful dog Fudgie the Chocolate Labrador. Now you can see why he is so special.
Shhh...
After a long adventurous day Fudgie loves to take a nap on his favorite spot on the couch.
Goodnight Fudgie.

The End.

Made in the USA
Lexington, KY
05 November 2014